CONKERS BONKERS!

Diane Wilmer

Illustrated by Paul Dowling

COLLINS

This is the story of Mr Nut
who doesn't like winter,
doesn't like spring,
doesn't even like summer,
but he *loves* autumn.

You might think he loves autumn
because of the falling rain and juicy,
ripe fruit.
Oh no!
Mr Nut loves autumn for one thing only . . .

CONKERS!
He is, quite simply, stark raving
CONKERS BONKERS!

Down at the bottom of Mr Nut's garden
there's an enormous horse-chestnut tree.
It's grown from a conker his great-grandaddy
planted one hundred and fifty years ago.

It's never been cut, pruned or trimmed
and every year it's taller and thicker
than the year before.

In the springtime when the tree
starts to shed its flowery candles
Mr Nut is on the look out for
teeny-tiny conkers.

He takes his deck-chair out into
the garden and sits staring up at
the baby conkers growing in the
sunshine.
"Conkers Bonkers!" yell the kids.
"Conkers Bonkers!" sniff the neighbours.
Mr Nut doesn't care.
Every day, all summer long, he sits
and watches and waits.

Then one autumn morning Mr Nut is
out in his garden, snoozing under the
tree, when BONK!
Something falls on his head.
"OUCH!" yelps Mr Nut.

Lying in his lap is a conker,
the first one to fall, and it's still
in its prickly green case.

Mr Nut squeezes it and out pops
the conker.
Smooth, brown, big and round.

"YIPPEE!" he shouts, and waits all
day for more to fall. But not one of them does.

They just hang there, fat and heavy
on the tree, waiting for the right moment.

As the days grow shorter and cooler,
the conkers begin to lose their hold
on the branches. They rattle and bounce
all over the garden. But Mr Nut always
finds them and he keeps every single one.

Now, when he sits in the garden, he wears a motor-bike helmet and holds a bucket between his knees.

"Come and get me, you beauties!" he roars
and whacks the tree with his rake.
The conkers shower down like rain-drops.
CLUNK ... PING ... BONG ... BONK!

Mr Nut laughs out loud as the conkers
bounce off his helmet and rattle into his bucket.
"Conkers Bonkers!" yell the kids.
"Conkers Bonkers!" sniff the neighbours.
But Mr Nut doesn't care.

As the autumn days pass fewer and
fewer conkers fall from the old
tree. But my goodness, you
should see the inside of Mr Nut's house!
He's got them in boxes, bags, bins, buckets
and barrels.

They're piled up on the telly,
lined along the window sills,
heaped onto shelves,
dotted around the carpet
and pouring out of the cellar.

As autumn comes to a chilly end, there's only one conker left at the top of the tree. The biggest, fattest, smoothest, brownest conker of them all!

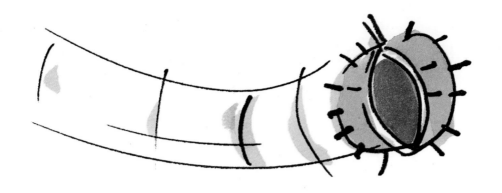

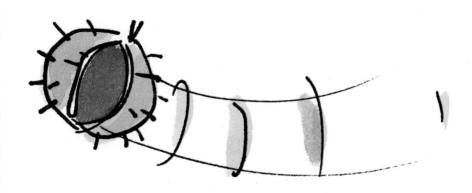

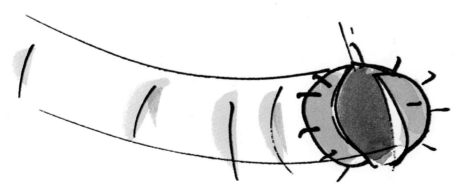

It hangs there, ripe and heavy.
Swinging back and forth . . .
back and forth . . . day . . . after . . .
day . . . after . . . day!

Mr Nut thinks that conker will drive him mad.

He wants it more than he's ever wanted anything, but he can't get at it!

He tries whacking the tree-trunk with the rake, but it doesn't work this time.

He tries shaking the tree with his bare hands.
"GRRRRRR!" that doesn't work either.

He tries climbing up, but it is too high.

He tries blowing it down.
"PHEWWW!"
But that's useless.

He tries jumping up and down and shouting at it.
"Come down here, you great, big, fat thing!"
That certainly doesn't work.

"Conkers Bonkers!" yell the kids.

"Conkers Bonkers!" sniff the neighbours.
"I DON'T CARE!" shrieks Mr Nut.
"I just want THAT conker."

And he wallops the tree with his big boot.

The conker wobbles and dithers . . .
Tumbles and slithers
   slowly
     through
       the leafy

     branches
       and lands
        at his
        feet

       bonk!

It's beautiful.
Mr Nut puts it in his pocket.
Then he runs indoors
and comes rushing out
with all his bags, buckets,
barrels and boxes of conkers.

"Here!" he yells to the kids.
"Have these."
"But . . . what about you?" they ask.

Mr Nut just smiles and holds out the last conker.
"I'm all right," he says. "I've got this one.
The biggest and the best of them all."